WILD BOG TEA

STORY BY

ANNETTE LEBOX

PICTURES BY

HARVEY CHAN

A GROUNDWOOD BOOK · DOUGLAS & McINTYRE
TORONTO VANCOUVER BUFFALO

THE BOG lay in the valley. I could see it from my bedroom window.

My grandfather called it a baby bog, for when he was a boy the land was still a marsh. Cattails grew around it, and ducks nested among the reeds.

He used to fish there, rowing a patched-up boat.

As the years passed, the marsh dried up. Moss crept along its edges, holding the still, green water in its spongy leaves. Then, layer by layer, peat formed, until slowly the marsh gave birth to the bog.

In time, a pair of sandhill cranes nested there. And at dawn and dusk, the valley was filled with singing.

On the day I was born, my grandfather discovered bog orchids growing among the sedges. He told me it was a sign, a celebration of my birth.

As soon as I could walk, my grandfather led me down the hill through a path in the forest to the baby bog.

There we breathed in the scent of sweet gale and wild plum. And we walked on carpets of red and green moss.

In the spring, we
watched the cranes dance
in the wet meadows. My
grandfather and I danced, too.

When it rained, my grandfather tucked
me under a salal bush to keep dry. I watched a
sundew plant catch insects while my grandfather
daydreamed.

Sometimes we played hide and seek. I learned
to curl up small and still, so my grandfather
couldn't find me.

On my eighth birthday, my grandfather gave me a pair of binoculars. That morning we went bird-watching in the bog. I saw my first little green heron that day.

When we were hungry, we picked wild cranberries. We ate the tart-sweet berries with cubes of sugar. And before we went home, we tucked sprigs of Labrador tea in our pockets.

Later, in the warmth of our kitchen, my grandfather made everyone wild bog tea.

In the spring, my grandfather and I saw deer lying among the mossy hummocks. And when the skunk cabbage bloomed, fawns were born. Overhead, eagles circled, announcing their birth.

By summer the sun baked the bog crisp and dry. And on hot nights, my grandfather and I carried our sleeping bags down to the valley. As we walked through the cool boggy air, moss crackled under our feet.

Above us, night owls skimmed the hardhack searching for voles. A coyote howled in the distance. The bog smelled of summer and happiness.

As the years passed, the forest moved closer and closer to the edge of the bog. Alder and dwarf lodgepole pine sprang up in the wet meadows.

"The bog is growing older," said my grandfather. "Long after we're gone, it will become forest."

When I grew up, I moved to the city. I loved the skyscrapers and sidewalk cafes and bright flashing lights. But I missed the baby bog and my grandfather.

So one day, I finally went home.

In my absence, my grandfather's hair had turned whiter, and his step had slowed.

"Let's walk to the baby bog," I said.

"The path is overgrown," replied my grandfather, "and the hill is too steep for me to climb."

So I went alone.

I breathed in the scent of sweet gale and wild plum. And I walked on red and green carpets of moss.

I watched the cranes dance in the wet meadows. And for the first time, I danced alone.

Before I left, I picked cranberries and tucked sprigs of Labrador tea in my pocket. Then I made my grandfather wild bog tea.

I told him that the bog laurel and the wild plum were in bloom.

I told him about the red-tailed hawk and the fawn I had seen.

My grandfather's eyes grew bright with hope.

"Next year..." he said.

I nodded and hugged him.

My grandfather left us that winter. But I have not forgotten him. When I go walking in the baby bog, I feel him beside me. He is there in the scent of sweet gale and wild plum.

He is there in the hummocks of bright red moss, soft and squishy under me.

He is there in the taste of wild bog tea.

AUTHOR'S NOTE

The setting of *Wild Bog Tea* is Blaney Bog, a wilderness wetland of approximately 146 hectares (360 acres) located in Maple Ridge, British Columbia. The area is composed of several distinct ecosystems: a grassy wetland called a fen, a tiny marsh (an area of low land that is flooded in wet weather), a bog and a forest.

A bog is an open wet place with few trees. Its water-logged soil holds very little oxygen and few nutrients. Bog plants have special ways of adapting to such poor growing conditions. The sundews learn to trap and digest insects as a source of nutrients. The fragrant leaves of Labrador tea are rolled and leathery with fuzzy undersides to conserve water. The leaves of bog laurel are also rolled, but they are narrower and shinier. The stems are thin and twisted. Bog laurel is poisonous. In the spring, the plant is covered with tiny pink star-shaped flowers, while Labrador tea has masses of white flowers.

Wild cranberry, bog rosemary, cloudberry and cottongrass are just a few of the special plants found in a bog. These are called indicator plants because they help identify an ecosystem as a bog.

Blaney Bog is home to threatened and endangered species such as the greater sandhill crane, the great blue heron, the green-backed heron, the American bittern and the peregrine falcon. Bear and deer also frequent the bog.

People in communities are born,

Bogs are places of natural beauty, but they also keep our environment healthy. Bogs absorb the carbon dioxide released by automobiles. By storing this pollutant in the peat, a bog helps prevent global warming. Digging up or draining a bog releases this carbon back into the air we breathe. Bogs also prevent flooding. The sphagnum holds water like a giant storage tank during wet periods, then slowly releases it during dry spells.

grow old and die. They change as they grow. Ecosystems change, too. Over time, the flow of water in a marsh or fen may slow down or grow stagnant. Less flow means less oxygen to break down dead plant material. These conditions encourage the growth of sphagnum moss, which is essential to the formation of a bog. Sphagnum soaks up water like a sponge and releases acid into the groundwater, killing the existing plants. The buildup of dead plant material forms peat. This is why bogs are sometimes called peatlands.

Sphagnum moss maintains the bog ecosystem by holding water in the soil, preventing trees from taking root. But if the water levels become too low, forest species such as salal, lodgepole pine and alder will take root in the peat. When this occurs, either through natural causes or human interference, the bog will begin its gradual transition to forest.

For Betty-Anne Hoff — AL

To my grandfathers whom
I wish I had known — HC

Text copyright © 2001 by Annette LeBox
Illustrations copyright © 2001 by Harvey Chan

Groundwood Books / Douglas & McIntyre
720 Bathurst Street, Suite 500, Toronto, Ontario M5S 2R4

Distributed in the USA by Publishers Group West
1700 Fourth Street, Berkeley, CA 94710

We acknowledge the financial support of the Canada Council for
the Arts, the Ontario Arts Council and the Government of Canada
through the Book Publishing Industry Development Program for
our publishing activities.

Canadian Cataloguing in Publication Data
LeBox, Annette
Wild bog tea
A Groundwood book.
ISBN 0-88899-406-0
I. Chan, Harvey. II. Title.
PS8573.E3364W54 2001   jC813.54   C00-931982-4
PZ7.L42Wi 2001

Book design by Michael Solomon
Printed and bound in China
by Everbest Printing Co. Ltd.